GOOD NIGHT, TRUCK

Sally Odgers ★ Heath McKenzie

FEIWEL AND FRIENDS
NEW YORK

A FEIWEL AND FRIENDS BOOK
An Imprint of Macmillan

This edition first published in the United States in 2016 by Feiwel and Friends.
First published by Scholastic Press, a division of Scholastic Australia Pty Limited, 2014.

Feiwel and Friends books may be purchased for business or promotional use.
For information on bulk purchases, please contact the Macmillan Corporate and Premium Sales Department
at (800) 221-7945 x5442 or by e-mail at specialmarkets@macmillan.com.

Library of Congress Cataloging-in-Publication Data
Odgers, Sally, 1957–
Good night, Truck / Sally Odgers ; illustrated by Heath McKenzie.
pages   cm
Summary: "A picture book about how trucks and other vehicles say good night"—Provided by publisher.
ISBN 978-1-250-07019-7 (hardback)
[1. Stories in rhyme. 2. Trucks—Fiction. 3. Vehicles—Fiction. 4. Bedtime—Fiction.] I. McKenzie, Heath, illustrator. II. Title.
PZ8.3.O284Go 2016   [E]—dc23   2015013380

Book design by Kimi Weart

Feiwel and Friends logo designed by Filomena Tuosto

First U.S. Edition: 2016

1 3 5 7 9 10 8 6 4 2

mackids.com

For Ashton and James, with love
—S. O.

For Ethan, Seb, and Damon
—H. M.

Hello, Truck! I'm on the road,
to haul a special heavy load.

We drive toward the rising sun
and toot the horn to everyone!

Hello, Digger! You're so strong.
Your engine roars a digging song.

We'll make a brand-new swimming pool.
My friends will think it's pretty cool.

Hello, Boat! You're sleek and fine, right and ready anytime.

Here's my hat! Just call me Skip.
I'll sail you on a harbor trip.

Hello, Tractor! Here's your plow.
I'm ready for some farming now.

Off we go! I'm very keen
to plant a crop of butter beans.

Hello, Rocket! Shall we fly? And write your name across the sky?

Up in space we swoop and zoom,
and off we'll race around the moon.

But rockets must come home at last,
when astronauts have traveled fast.
The rocket pod is here on Mars.
"Good night, Rocket," sing the stars.

The fields are neatly plowed in rows
for lots of butter beans to grow.
I'll drive you to the tractor shed.
Good night, Tractor. Time for bed.

The harbor trip was lots of fun.
We sailed toward the setting sun.

It's nearly teatime by the clock.
Good night, Boat. You're safely docked.

We've finished digging for the day.
In the morning, we can play.

Here's a garage you can use.
Good night, Digger. Time to snooze.

Now I'm cozy in my bed.
Snuggle down, you sleepyhead.

There's one more friend I need to tuck. . . .

He's here beside me.
Good night, Truck.